MEG'S CAR

for Thomas

MEG'S CAR

by Helen Nicoll
and Jan Pieńkowski

PUFFIN BOOKS

Cuckoo

It was a lovely day
for a picnic

Meg Mog and Owl
wanted to go
in a car

So Meg made a spell

Boot and bonnet
Rattle and clang
Make me a car
That goes with a bang

CLA
CLINK

CLUNK
NK

Everybody's dream

had almost come true

They all piled into the new car

Mog
started
the
engine

The car shot backwards

into a tree

then
lurched
forward

and sped off down the road

It went with a bolt and a jolt

a thump, a bump and a jump

and
stopped

CLANG

It needs petrol
It needs oil
Just add an egg

The car started
off,
took
It

the air
through
flew

and landed

in a tree

So they went to the picnic
on the broomstick

Goodbye!